Annie and Snowball and the Dress-up Birthday

The First Book of Their Adventures

Cynthia Rylant

Illustrated by Suçie Stevenson

Ready-to-Read
ALADDIN PAPERBACKS
New York   London   Toronto   Sydney

For Jane Stevenson
—S. S.

ALADDIN PAPERBACKS
An imprint of Simon & Schuster Children's Publishing Division
1230 Avenue of the Americas, New York, NY 10020

Also available in a Simon & Schuster
Books for Young Readers hardcover edition.
Designed by Jessica Sonkin
The text of this book was set in Goudy.
The illustrations for this book were rendered in pen-and-ink and watercolor.
Manufactured in the United States of America
First Aladdin Paperbacks edition April 2008
2 4 6 8 10 9 7 5 3 1
The Library of Congress has cataloged the hardcover edition as follows:
Rylant, Cynthia.
Annie and Snowball and the dress-up birthday / Cynthia Rylant ;
illustrated by Suçie Stevenson.—1st ed.
p. cm.
Summary: Annie and her pet rabbit, Snowball, invite
Henry and Mudge to a dress-up birthday party, but there
is some confusion about what the guests are supposed to wear.
ISBN-13: 978-1-4169-0938-5 (hc)
ISBN-10: 1-4169-0938-9 (hc)
[1. Birthdays—Fiction. 2. Parties—Fiction. 3. Rabbits—Fiction.]
I. Stevenson, Suçie, ill. II. Title.
PZ7.R982Ann 2007
[E]—dc22
2006002516
ISBN-13: 978-1-4169-1459-4 (pbk)
ISBN-10: 1-4169-1459-5 (pbk)

Contents

Favorite Things

It was almost Annie's birthday,
and Annie was very excited.
On birthdays Annie got to wear
her favorite things:
ribbons and bows and lace
and fancy little shoes.

This year she had her new bunny,
Snowball.
She would dress up Snowball, too!
Annie couldn't wait.

Annie decided she wanted to celebrate
her birthday with just her family.
Her family was her dad and Snowball,
of course.

But Annie's family was
also her cousin Henry,
Henry's parents,
and Henry's big dog,
Mudge.

Annie had moved next door
to Henry and Mudge, and she loved it.

They watched old movies and
ate popcorn on Friday nights.
They threw Frisbees.
They played board games.

11

And, of course, Annie and Henry
spoiled each other's pets.
Annie adored Mudge.
She gave him good brushings.

And Henry liked Snowball.

He gave her good scratchings.

It was so much fun living side by side!

So Annie decided to have a nice, quiet
birthday with her family.
She'd ask everyone to dress up.
It would be great!

Dress-up Plans

Annie telephoned Henry.
Henry and Mudge were cleaning
Henry's fish tank.
Henry was cleaning, and Mudge
was handling the spills.

When Henry answered the phone,
Annie told him that Tuesday was
her birthday.

"Dad is going to make my favorite foods," said Annie.

"Finger sandwiches and lemon tarts and strawberries dipped in chocolate."

"Yum," said Henry, scrubbing his castle.
Mudge was wiping up the floor.

"And it's going to be
a Dress-up Birthday," said Annie.
"Great!" said Henry.
"Tell your parents, okay?" said Annie.
"Sure!" said Henry.
Annie and Henry said good-bye.

Annie imagined what she would wear
for her Dress-up Birthday.
And she couldn't wait to dress up
Snowball!

Next door Henry imagined
what he would wear.
And he couldn't wait to dress up
Mudge!
Annie's birthday would be fun!

A Happy Day

Tuesday came and Annie's house
looked beautiful.
Annie's dad had filled it with daisies
and carnations and yellow balloons.

Annie looked beautiful too.
She had dressed up in her best satin
dress and sparkly pink tights and little
white gloves with pearls.

Snowball also looked nice.
She had lacy ears and a glittery nose
and a little blue bow on her tail.

Even Annie's dad looked special.

He was in a tuxedo.

(Annie had asked.)

Finally the doorbell rang.
"That must be Henry!" said Annie.
Annie and Snowball and Annie's dad
opened the door.

And there stood a pirate, a gypsy,
a mummy, and a moose.
For a moment everybody just stared.

Then the pirate said to Annie,
"I thought you told me this was
a dress-up party."
"It is," said Annie.

"Well, I thought you meant costumes," the pirate said as one of the moose's antlers fell off.

33

"Gee," said the mummy, "I did put on
my best bandages."
Everyone laughed and laughed.

Then they all had a lovely party.
The mummy served the tarts,
and the pretend moose
and the bunny cleaned
up the crumbs.

Annie got a new teacup,
a pretty doll,
and a special set
of little china plates.

Then when everything was finished,
the gypsy told everyone's fortunes.

She told Annie that all of Annie's days
would be as happy as this one.

But Annie already knew that.
Because she had Snowball
and Henry and Mudge
as her very best friends!